For Valia —

Happy Birthday

with love & hugs

Shendra

MW01056598

ALL THE STARS IN THE SKY

Native Stories from the Heavens

C.J. TAYLOR

Tundra Books

For my grandson, Shayne

Text and illustrations copyright © 2006 by C.J. Taylor

Published in Canada by Tundra Books,
75 Sherbourne Street, Toronto, Ontario M5A 2P9

Published in the United States by Tundra Books of Northern New York,
P.O. Box 1030, Plattsburgh, New York 12901

Library of Congress Control Number: 2005911001

All rights reserved. The use of any part of this publication reproduced, transmitted in any form or by any means, electronic, mechanical, photocopying, recording, or otherwise, or stored in a retrieval system, without the prior written consent of the publisher – or, in case of photocopying or other reprographic copying, a licence from the Canadian Copyright Licensing Agency – is an infringement of the copyright law.

Library and Archives Canada Cataloguing in Publication

Taylor, C. J. (Carrie J.), 1952-
    All the stars in the sky : Native stories from the heavens / C.J. Taylor.

ISBN 13: 978-0-88776-759-3   ISBN 10: 0-88776-759-1

    1. Indians of North America – Juvenile fiction.   2. Children's stories, Canadian (English). I. Title.

PS8589.A88173A64 2006   jc813'.54   C2005-907472-8

ONTARIO ARTS COUNCIL
CONSEIL DES ARTS DE L'ONTARIO

We acknowledge the financial support of the Government of Canada through the Book Publishing Industry Development Program (BPIDP) and that of the Government of Ontario through the Ontario Media Development Corporation's Ontario Book Initiative. We further acknowledge the support of the Canada Council for the Arts and the Ontario Arts Council for our publishing program.

The illustrations for this book were rendered in acrylics
Design: Kong Njo

Printed and bound in China

1 2 3 4 5 6   11 10 09 08 07 06

CONTENTS

LiTTLe mouse aND ThE maGic cirCLeS

OJIBWA
Woodlands and Central North America

White Hawk was a good hunter. He spent much time traveling the prairies in search of game. One day he came upon a strange sight: a patch of grass that looked as if it had been worn down by many feet. Yet he found no path to or from the circle.

He spent the day thinking and wondering about the curious circle in the grass.

"Perhaps it is star people that have made this circle," he thought.

Night was falling so he hid himself away in the tall, fragrant grass that stood around the circle. As the sky drew darker and the stars began their nightly dance across the heavens, White Hawk fell asleep.

The night was still black when he was awakened by the faint sound of music. He turned his eyes skyward and saw a small shining speck, coming closer and closer. The music grew louder and louder. As the light neared White Hawk's hiding place, he saw that the sparkling speck was, in fact, a wondrously made round basket. It came to rest soundlessly on the circle grass.

One by one, twelve oddly beautiful young women emerged from the basket. Little Hawk realized that the music he had heard was the sound of their singing. With stately steps they danced, around and around the circle. White Hawk was dazzled. When his eyes fell upon the youngest of the dancing sisters, he was seized with passion for her delicate beauty. As she danced near him, he sprang from his hiding place. But she was too quick. She stepped aside nimbly and she and her sisters rushed to their brilliant round basket and ascended into the heavens. Poor White Hawk was heartbroken.

The next day he returned to his village. Many days passed, yet he could not stop thinking of the heavenly creature. Each night he dreamed of the delicate young maiden who had taken his heart.

When he could stand the torment no longer, White Hawk returned to the enchanted circle. He wandered around its edge, his thoughts on his beloved. As he made his way through the tall grass, he came upon a hollow log. It was home to a nest of field mice. Beside the log lay a small deerskin pouch, tied to a long string. White Hawk held it in his hand. All at once he knew what he must do to end his torment, for the pouch held strong magic.

White Hawk once again hid himself among the grasses at the circle's edge and waited for night to fall.

He did not have to wait long. Again, the stars began their nightly dance across the heavens, and again, White Hawk heard the faint sound of strange, unearthly music. Looking up he saw the tiny speck speeding towards him. Closer and closer it came. Louder and louder grew the voices of the beautiful star creatures within their wondrous basket. When the sparkling basket gently came to rest in the center of the circle, twelve sisters once again came out and danced in the circle to the rhythm of their music.

With the long string, White Hawk tied the magic pouch around his neck. The moment he did so, he turned into a little mouse. As his beloved twirled by, the field mice ran from their hollow log into the circle. The maidens stopped dancing and watched the mice scamper about in the starlight. All but one little mouse. It sat still at the feet of White Hawk's beloved. Being curious as well as lovely, she picked up the furry animal. "Who are you, my tiny friend?" she asked.

Suddenly, the little mouse changed back into a handsome young man. "My name is White Hawk." Immediately the star maiden was smitten. The others, though, were frightened by the man who'd appeared among them. They ran back to the sparkling round basket, calling out to their sister to follow them.

It was no use. The star maiden chose to stay with the handsome young man. Her eleven sisters returned to the starworld. White Hawk and his beloved returned to the village.

Everyone welcomed White Hawk's new bride. They gave her a name – Star Woman. Time passed and Star Woman quickly learned the ways of the people. She was content, but often she thought with longing of her sky home, her sisters, and most of all, Grandfather Star.

She missed them more and more after the birth of a son, Sky Bird. As the child grew older, he asked many questions about his relatives in the starworld. The day came when Star Woman was overcome with homesickness. Taking Sky Bird and the magic pouch, she left the village and returned to the circle of flattened grass. She wove a round basket from the long reeds that grew by the edge of the circle. She hung the magic pouch around Sky Bird's neck, and picking up the child, she climbed inside the basket. She raised her voice in song. The basket began to glow. And then, it floated toward the heavens.

Star Woman was content to be home. Everyone welcomed her and her child. Grandfather Star was happiest of all, and pleased to have such a fine grandson. But soon Star Woman's contentment was replaced with a terrible longing for her husband, White Hawk. She knew her son missed his father, too.

White Hawk also grieved for his lost family. Every day he returned to the enchanted circle. There he waited and waited. Finally, Grandfather Star could not bear the suffering of the three. He spoke to Star Woman. "I see the pain you carry, Granddaughter. Go and bring White Hawk to me. On your return, bring earthly gifts for your star relatives."

That night, as White Hawk sat forlorn in the enchanted circle, he heard a faint sound from above. As it grew closer and clearer, he recognized the voices of Star Woman and Sky Bird singing.

Overjoyed at their return, he joined in their singing. The family was whole again.

When Star Woman told her husband of Grandfather's invitation to the starworld and his request for earthly gifts, White Hawk eagerly agreed. The three fell to work, gathering gifts of colorful flowers and healing plants. They made bundles of feathers, antlers, quills, and many other treasures and piling them all into the round sparkling basket, they climbed in and set off for the starworld.

The star people were delighted with the gifts White Hawk and his family brought. Grandfather permitted each to choose one. When, at last, all the gifts were spoken for, White Hawk took three of the four white feathers from his hair. He gave one to Sky Bird, one to Star Woman, and the last to Grandfather Star.

Grandfather Star held the feather solemnly. "Never again shall you be apart." With a great sweeping motion he waved the feather over their heads. Suddenly, White Hawk, Star Woman, and Sky Bird changed into three magnificent hawks. They flew down to the earth together. You can still see them today as they fly over the prairies.

OSE

Rocky Mounta...   ...nd British Columbia

The constellation kn... ws the path of the Milky Way. To the Salish of the ... constellation is known as the Great Snow Goose.

Deep in the lus... ains to the west, there was a magical lake. ... and clear. This peaceful lake held all the colors ... day, insects shimmered and buzzed as they glide... ripples through the reflected shoreline. Mirrored ... floating clouds. Within the lake's calm bounda... selves building homes and raising their young ... e of night creatures echoed across the star-silve...

The most magi... hat came to this enchanted place was Snow Go... ble bird of great beauty and all that inhabited t... ted it. Even the water itself

Butterflies— one of nature's most beloved creatures

Butterflies and Butterfly Gardening IN THE PACIFIC NORTHWEST

MARY KATE WOODWARD

PUBLISHED BY WHITECAP

DISTRIBUTED BY FIREFLY BOOKS

ISBN 1-55285-707-7

hitecap | www.whitecap.ca

PRINTED IN CANADA

welcomed the majestic bird. To mirror such grace, such beauty, was indeed, an honor.

Late one afternoon as Sun sent its last rays of light through the trees to dance across the waters, three brothers out hunting came across a steep trail leading to the lake. This pathway had been made and used by the creatures of the forest. No human had ever traveled its intricate twists and turns. Now, the youngest of the brothers was called Itchy Foot. He was always impatient, anxious to rush ahead, often without thinking. His impulsive nature had lost them much game on the hunt. Itchy Foot sprinted ahead up the difficult path, leaving his older brothers behind.

"Slow down, little brother," called Many Winds. He stopped to wait for the eldest brother, Growling Bear.

"He is well-named, that one," said Growling Bear when he finally caught up.

"As are you, brother." Many Winds liked to tease his serious brother.

Many Winds realized he could no longer see or hear his young brother. He called out, "Itchy Foot, do you hear me? Wait where you are." There was no reply.

Many Winds was worried as he picked his way up the treacherous path as quickly as he could. Growling Bear followed close behind, grumbling all the while. It was growing dark as the two came to the end of the trail. There they found Itchy Foot. He was standing before a narrow gap that tunneled through the thick undergrowth. Through the gap lights flickered, bright red and yellow, green, and purple and blue.

Before Many Winds and Growling Bear could tell their brother that it would be best to wait for morning to investigate, Itchy Foot disappeared into the crude, overgrown tunnel. The two brothers had no choice but to follow.

Sun sank behind the tree-topped horizon as the three brothers crawled through the tunnel. It led them to a beautiful lake. The water reflected the last of Sun's light in glorious colors. A tall, rocky cliff jutted out of the ever-rippling waters. The mirrored trees along the shoreline danced across the gentle waves that lapped the sandy shore where the three brothers stood.

Suddenly a new reflection appeared on the waters. It circled, growing larger. The brothers looked up to see a giant white bird. The graceful bird came to rest upon the lake's surface and its great beauty was reflected so that the brothers were awestruck by its splendor.

Growling Bear was the first to find his voice. "We have come upon a sacred place. There is strong magic here."

"We must show respect to the waters and all that live here," said Many Winds.

Hearing nothing from Itchy Foot, the two turned to find that he had, once again, disappeared. They searched the beach and shoreline and finally they spotted him, high on the rocky cliff overlooking the lake. He raised his bow and arrow and took aim.

Growling Bear and Many Winds called out, but their brother took no notice.

"I will show them who is the best hunter," he said, fitting an arrow into his bow.

Startled by the commotion, the great bird spread its huge, white wings and rose into the air. Itchy Foot's arrow flew from his bow. It met its mark, driving through the soft white feathers and piercing the heart of the noble bird. It fell from the sky into the lake.

As it sank below the surface, all the colors of the waters faded away. The lake grew dark and still. Itchy Foot could do nothing but watch.

"What have I done?" he cried.

On the beach, Growling Bear and Many Winds asked the same question. "What has he done?"

From the dark silence came the soft keening of the night creatures. The still waters slowly began to keep rhythm. Night stars came out to dance across the gentle waves. The three brothers looked toward the sky and saw the spirit of the giant bird, its great white wings spread wide, as it flew up into the heavens.

And that is where it lives to this day – the magnificent Snow Goose – winging across the sky in the dark of night.

THERE THEY LIVE IN PEACE

ONONDAGA
Woodlands of Eastern North America

The constellation known as Pleides has inspired many legends across the world's cultures. North American myths vary as widely as the nations that tell them. The Blackfoot version tells of a boy's revenge for not receiving yellow buffalo calf robes. The Nez Perces call the stars the seven sisters. This is the Onondaga story of dancing children known to them as oot-kwa-tah.

One autumn long ago, a chief led his people through the stately woodlands of the northeast. They were in search of new hunting grounds and a place to build their village. As they traveled deeper into the great forest, they came upon a beautiful lake. Many streams flowed into it and it was abundant with fish. Deer came to the shore to drink the cool, clear waters. Morning and evening, bears came to take their morning meals of fish. In the hills surrounding the lake, there grew tall chestnut, beech, and maple trees.

The chief looked upon this land of plenty and spoke to the people. "Let us give thanks to the Creator for guiding us to our new home. This is where we shall build our village."

Everyone fell to clearing the trees and building the longhouses. Men hunted and women gathered food for the long winter ahead. All were so busy that the children were left to make their own amusement.

One day, they wandered away from the village and found a secluded beach. From then on, the children gathered together to dance and sing, every day becoming more boisterous. The soft, sandy beach was marred with footprints from their wild dancing. And then, while the children sang their songs and danced their dances, a strange old man appeared at the wood's edge behind the beach. He wore a robe of gleaming white feathers. His hair, shining silver, floated about his shoulders. His face held the many wrinkles of time.

"I am the Spirit and the Guardian of the Forest." His voice was harsh. "You children show no respect for the tranquility of my beautiful beach. Your footprints scar the sand and your clamor frightens the animals and birds. Go home at once, before something terrible happens."

As suddenly as the Spirit of the Forest had appeared, he vanished.

The children paid little heed to his warning. They danced and sang even more wildly, as each day passed, and each day, the Spirit of the Forest appeared to warn them.

One day, as they gathered at the secluded beach, a certain little boy who was very fond of eating said, "Tomorrow let us bring food from home so we may feast after we dance." When they all returned to their lodges each child asked for something to take to the feast. The parents refused. "We are too busy." "You will waste food." "Come home to eat as you should."

The next day the children returned to the beach to dance and sing as usual. Again the Spirit of the Forest came to warn them. Still, they continued to pay no attention. It was not long before their heads felt light and their empty stomachs ached. Little by little, they found themselves leaving the ground and rising into the sky.

As he floated higher and higher, one boy cried out, "Do not look back!"

A mother from the village saw the children floating away and she called to them, but they kept rising skyward. She hurried to tell the other parents. As quickly as they could, they snatched up food and rushed to the beach, calling their children's names. But the children continued their skyward journey.

One little girl who could not resist looking down at her mother's face, changed into a falling star. The others, upon reaching the heavens, turned into stars.

That night as Grandmother Moon came out to welcome her bright new stars, the old Spirit of the Forest stood on his secluded beach. "*Oot-kwa-tah!*" he called out. "There, they will live in peace."

OLD MAN STEALS SUN'S LEGGINGS

BLACKFOOT
The Great Plains

One day, Old Man was wandering about the world making things like mountains and lakes, rolling plains, and beautiful trees. By midday he had reached the top of the world and he'd worked up quite an appetite.

Sun's lodge was close by, so Old Man decided to pay a visit. *Perhaps he will have a tasty treat or two for me*, he thought.

Old Man arrived at the lodge to find Sun preparing for the hunt.

"There is nothing left in my cooking skin. Would you care to join me in the hunt? Then we shall both feast," said Sun, reaching up for a bundle hanging above his sleeping skins.

Old Man always enjoyed hunting. "I would be delighted to join you," he said, curious about the bundle Sun was unrolling. In it was the most splendid pair of leggings Old Man had ever seen. They were made of the softest white hide. Fine quillwork, each quill dyed to match Sun's hair in bright yellows, reds, and oranges traced the side seams. Old Man watched Sun pull on the leggings. "Those are very fine," he said.

"Thank you, my friend. They are indeed very beautiful and they hold much magic."

"What magic can leggings hold?" asked Old Man.

"You will see," said Sun. He picked up his arrows and led the way into the forest. "You will see."

They soon came upon a herd of deer grazing in an open meadow. Old Man watched as Sun silently raised his bow and took careful aim. "Work your magic, leggings, for I am hungry." Sun's voice was no more than a whisper.

Suddenly flames shot from the bright quillwork that ran down the sides of the leggings. The flames burned a path through the grass, surrounding the herd of deer and sending them directly into Sun's flying arrow. As suddenly as the flames appeared they were gone, leaving the grass untouched. Sun's arrow had met its mark. Old Man and Sun would feast.

Old Man was amazed. The leggings were indeed magic.

That evening, after both had eaten their fill, Sun said, "Old Man, you are welcome to share my lodge for the night before you continue your travels tomorrow."

"Your invitation is very gracious. I accept." All the while Old Man was thinking, *I must have these magic leggings.*

Sun was very tired so he prepared for bed. Carefully he rolled up the magic leggings and hung them above his sleeping skins. It was not long before he was fast asleep. When Old Man heard Sun's loud snores, he crept over and unhooked the rolled-up bundle that contained the magic leggings. All through the dark night he ran, clutching the bundle. As the sky began to grow light, Old Man finally stopped to rest. He placed the magic leggings under his head. *I will close my eyes, just for a moment.* But he fell into a deep sleep.

Old Man was wakened by a loud voice. "Why are my leggings under your head?"

Old Man had run all night across the world, only to find himself back in Sun's lodge. He did not want to admit the theft, so Old Man said, "Oh, in the middle of the night I needed a pillow. I didn't want to disturb you. In the dark, I found this bundle." He handed the magic leggings to Sun. "Because half my night was spent without a pillow, I did not sleep well. I need another day's rest before I continue my travels."

Sun was a good host. He could not refuse.

That night, Old Man waited again to hear Sun's loud snoring. In the darkness he snatched the bundle hanging over Sun's sleeping skins and ran into the night. He ran over tall mountains, through dense forests, along the shores of long, winding rivers. When the sky grew light, Old Man sat down. "Surely I am far enough away that I may rest for awhile." And once more he fell into a deep sleep.

"Old Man, why are my magic leggings under your head?" Sun's voice startled Old Man awake. Just like before, he was back where he had started. Not waiting for an answer, Sun said, "Old Man, you have forgotten. The whole earth is my lodge. You cannot possibly run from me. If you wish to have my leggings so badly, I give them to you. But be careful. They are very powerful."

Old Man was so excited, he didn't hear Sun's words of caution. He grabbed the bundle of magic leggings and left, not even remembering to thank Sun for his hospitality or his gift.

Old Man continued on his journey across the earth, the magic leggings tucked away in his travel bundle. He thought about them all day as he worked, making things. By day's end, Old Man was finishing up his work on a river that ran from the high mountains into a huge lake. Standing at the top, he poured great amounts of water into the dry river bed. "Just one more thing," he said. He bent down and placed a small island in the center of the lake. Old Man stood up and looked over his creation.

"Perfect, but all this work has made me very hungry." He remembered having seen a herd of deer in a thicket not far from the lake. *I will use my new magic leggings*, he thought. He unrolled the bundle and pulled on the magnificent leggings. He found the deer just where he had remembered. Taking careful aim with his bow, he said softly, "Work your magic, leggings, for I am hungry."

Fire shot from the fine quillwork that ran down his legs. The earth around his feet burst into flames that quickly encircled him. The fire grew bigger and hotter. Smoke blurred Old Man's vision. He dropped his bow and arrow and tried to stomp out the spreading flames that surrounded him. It was useless. The fire burned hotter and higher. There was nothing to do but run. Old Man took great loping strides toward the lake, flames shooting from the magic leggings, igniting everything in his path. He thought he would never reach the lake. When he finally reached its shores he made one giant leap into the water, sending great crashing waves over its burning tree-lined banks. The fire was out.

Old Man sat in the cooling waters. Great billows of smoke came from his blackened and burnt leggings and curled around his head. As the waters calmed, Sun appeared over the distant trees. "Be careful what you wish for, Old Man," he laughed. "Be careful what you wish for."

SHAMAN VISITS MOON

NETSILIK (INUIT)
Far North

The mid-winter evening air was crisp. Moon shone brightly, surrounded by millions of stars. The blue-white glow lit the snow-covered ice. The snow squeaked under Shaman's sealskin boots as he prepared his harpoon. The bitter cold made his fingers numb and ate through his heavy skin coat and pants, sending shivers through his body. With difficulty he hooked the rope in place along the length of his harpoon and slipped his frozen hands into his fur-lined mitts. He twisted one end of the rope around his mittened hand and stood before the breathing hole in the ice. Shaman looked up at Moon and the sparkling stars and spoke.

"Thank you, Moon, for your light. You have made my task easier on such a cold night. My family is hungry. Perhaps this breathing hole will provide a nice fat seal. It is good to have your company while I wait."

As Shaman spoke, Moon began to move. At first slowly, then faster and faster. Closer and closer came Moon. Shaman stood frozen, not from cold, but by what he saw.

Moon approached, growing larger and brighter. The winds came howling across the skies and the vast frozen horizon carrying great sheets of swirling snow. Through the vale of bright white, Shaman saw a huge sled pulled by three enormous dogs, speeding toward him.

The sled team was driven by a giant of a man. His fur coat and pants were as white as the snow. The sled came closer and closer. Shaman heard a voice bellowing through the winds, reining in the fearsome dogs a short distance from the breathing hole and Shaman. As the sled came to a stop, so did the howling winds and driving snow. Shaman saw that the giant man was Moon himself.

Moon called out to Shaman, "Come! Get on my sled." As Shaman crawled into the gigantic sled, Moon told him, "Keep your eyes shut."

At once, the dogs shot off skyward. Shaman tried to peek, but the bitter wind, the snow, and great speed, forced his eyes closed tight. He could feel and hear the sounds of the sled runners on the snow beneath him. He heard Moon roar commands to the dogs, and the sled slid to a stop. Shaman opened his eyes. Spread before him stood a huge village, full of the finest white hide tents. He saw people waving to him. Many he recognized. Shaman realized he stood in the Land of the Dead, far off in the sky.

"Come to my home," said Moon. He strode quickly to the largest igloo Shaman had ever seen. He had to trot to keep up with the giant.

Shaman could see that the igloo was well built. Its surface was smooth and cast a blue-white light, as if a thousand oil lamps burned inside. At the entrance slept the biggest of the dogs. As Moon and Shaman approached, the dog sat up. He strained at his harness, growling and showing his long white fangs. Moon motioned to the dog and he returned to his napping.

Moon stooped to crawl through the doorway. As Shaman followed close behind, the passageway began to change. The snow blocks looked like giant teeth. The smooth floor started heaving up and down. It was like walking in a gigantic, chewing mouth.

They came upon another passageway. Its entrance was covered with an enormous white hide. Moon pulled it aside and crawled through, motioning to Shaman to follow.

Shaman looked around and saw there were not a thousand oil lamps lighting the igloo. The walls were not made of smooth snow blocks like the outside. They were covered with beautiful glowing white hides that shimmered with light. At the farthest end of the lodge was another passage. Its hide-covered entry glittered with colors Shaman had never seen. There was a welcoming warmth that seemed to call to him.

Moon pulled aside the glowing hide. "I share my lodge with my sister, Sun." Behind the hide sat a beautiful young woman holding a small child. Beside her there burned an oil lamp, the flame so high and hot, it scorched Shaman's sealskin coat and burned his eyes. Yet he could not look away.

"Welcome to our home, Shaman," she said, smiling. "Come sit here by my lamp. I will fill a bowl with the best seal meat for you. You will never be cold or hungry again."

Shaman thought about his family; his beautiful wife, and the two small children who depended on him. They would starve. There would be no oil to heat their snow lodge. The children would not have warm coats or boots made from the furs of the animals he hunted. They would wait forever for his return, not knowing what had happened. Shaman knew that if he stayed any longer and ate of the Sun's seal meat, he would forget about his family.

Quickly he turned from Sun, and ran through the hanging hides, past
Moon, into the giant chewing maw of a passage, and past the fearsome
sleeping dog. Following the path past the white hide tents and waving relatives and friends he had lost, but longed to see again, Shaman came to the
place where the trail turned from ice to snow. He shut his eyes tight and
jumped. He fell down, down, down.

Shaman awoke to find himself back at the breathing hole. Something
was tugging at him. The harpoon rope twisted around his hand and tugged
again. Quickly Shaman drew in his harpoon line. On its end was a fat seal.

But he did not forget his visit with Moon. Shaman looked skyward.
"Thank you Moon for your company. My family waits. This seal will feed
them. It will heat our lodge. And as my wife sews the children's new coats,
I will tell them stories of our visit."

COYOTE CREATES THE BIG DIPPER

WASCO
Western Rockies

It was Coyote who placed the stars in the night sky. He was very proud of his work. "I am a fine artist," he would brag to anyone who would listen, his nose pointing to the heavens.

One evening, Coyote was taking a leisurely stroll and admiring the sparkling points of light overhead when he noticed an empty black space near the Bear Star. When he got to the top of his favorite mountain, a spot where he could see the whole universe, he sat down for a moment. He turned his head from side to side. "I shall have to think about this," he said. Coyote continued his evening stroll, deep in thought.

Soon he came upon a pack of wolves and their dog. They were sitting on a cliff, their noses pointing skyward. They were discussing the Bear Star. Now, sometimes Coyote is very sneaky. He hid behind a tree to watch and listen.

"It is impossible to hunt a bear so far away," said one of the wolves. "Let us be on our way."

Suddenly Coyote had an idea. As the wolves and their dog turned to leave, he jumped out from his hiding place. "Hello cousins. I noticed you admiring the Bear Star. He is indeed a fine bear."

"Yes, it is true, cousin." The largest of the wolves stepped forward. "But he is too far away, and there is no trail for us to follow. We will take our hunt elsewhere."

"I can help you," Coyote boasted, sitting down in front of the wolf, his bushy tail curled around his skinny front legs. "Sometimes, cousin, your assistance is more trouble than it's worth," replied the wolf. Everyone knew how much Coyote liked to play tricks.

"I only wish to help my relatives." Coyote moved aside as the wolves and their dog made their way down the trail. "It is such a fine bear and you are such good hunters. What a shame!" The pack stopped and gazed skyward. It was indeed a fine bear.

"What do you propose, Coyote?" asked the leader. "We want none of your tricks, mind you," he warned, baring his long white fangs.

"Of course not," said Coyote.

They all gathered around to hear Coyote's plan. "As you know, cousins, it was I who placed the stars in the skyworld. So, does it not make sense that I would know the trail?"

The wolves and dog agreed. "All right, we will follow your trail," said the leader, not quite trusting his crafty cousin.

"First I must fetch my travel bundle," said Coyote. He dashed off into the woods. Just as quickly, he returned with a tattered bundle. He unrolled the old hide. Before them lay a bent and badly strung bow and several crooked arrows. Coyote proudly announced, "This is our trail.

These are magic arrows. I will shoot them into the sky and we will climb up to the Bear."

The pack leader showed his teeth. "You take us for fools, Coyote. Such bent and twisted arrows are useless." The other wolves and the dog began to growl and snap their teeth. The hair stood up on their backs.

Sometimes Coyote can think fast. "It is the same trail Bear used. The bow and arrows may seem bent and crooked but they are shaped to fit my arms."

The wolves and dog gave that some thought. They growled amongst themselves.

"Well, if you are not interested, no harm done. I will be on my way." Coyote started to bundle up the crooked arrows and the bent bow. As if speaking to himself, he muttered, "It is such a shame. Such a fine bear. A nice fat bear like that would feed a family for a long time."

Holding the bundle he paused to gaze skyward. "Yes, a shame. Oh, well. Good hunting to you, cousins." As he turned to leave, Coyote heard more growling. This time it was their stomachs.

"Hold on, Coyote. We did not mean to doubt you. Being hungry makes us short-tempered. Please show us the trail," said the leader.

"Very well," replied Coyote. "But you must listen to my instructions. We may be in for danger."

Once more, he unrolled the tattered bundle. He reached for the bent bow and one of the crooked arrows. He took careful aim. The arrow twisted and turned toward the sky and held fast in a cloud that misted over the mountain tops. One after another the arrows whizzed from Coyote's bow. Each was planted firmly in the clouds until a ladder had formed right up to

Bear Star. In great amazement the wolves and dog shouted, "This time Coyote's magic works!" They climbed the ladder trail skyward.

Coyote led the way. When he reached the last arrow near the Bear Star, he stopped. "This is where you must follow my instructions carefully," he told the leader, the largest of the wolves. "Step into the sky. Dog, you follow, then the rest." All took their places, waiting for further instructions, as Coyote pranced up and down the shaft of the top arrow. "No, No. That's not right." He pointed to each. "You, go over there. You, go there." The wolves and dog ran every which way, becoming more and more confused. By the time Coyote shouted, "That's it. Perfect!" they were worn out.

The leader called out, "Let us sit awhile and watch Bear while we rest." But soon the wolves and the dog fell asleep. Coyote quickly descended the trail, pulling out each arrow as he ran, dropping a few along the way. When he reached the earth he returned to his favorite mountaintop from where he could see the whole universe. His tail curled around the bent arrows. When he looked up into the night sky at the Bear Star, there sat the wolves and their dog, and there they would hunt Bear forever. Turning his head from side to side Coyote said, "I am a wonderful artist, and clever too!"

GRANDMOTHER SPIDER BRINGS LIGHT

CHEROKEE
East Tennessee, North Carolina, Northern Georgia

In the beginning, only half the world had light. The other half lived in darkness. The people, animals and birds who lived without light were not happy. They could not see anything. There were many accidents, many bumpings into trees and bushes, and even into each other.

Everyone came together – the people, the animals, and the birds – to discuss what might be done.

The people were the first to speak. "We need light. Does anyone know where we might find some?"

Fox came forward. "I have heard of a place on the other side of the world that has plenty of light. But the people there are greedy. They will not give any away."

The discussion went on and on, nobody knows for how long. It was difficult to measure time without day and night.

Finally Possum came up with a plan. "As everyone knows, I have a very beautiful bushy tail. I will steal a tiny piece of light and hide it in my fur.

I will return with it before the people even realize that some of their light is missing."

All agreed. Possum's tail was, indeed, a fine bushy one. "It could work," they said.

Possum set out for the other side of the world. He traveled a great distance until he came upon the tallest of all trees. At the very top hung a huge ball of light, glowing brighter than anything Possum had ever seen. Quickly, he climbed the tree. The closer he came to the brilliant ball of light, the hotter it became, until it burned his tiny toes. He dashed forward, grabbed a scrap of light, and stuffed it into the fur of his bushy tail. As he climbed down the tall tree, he noticed gray, smelly smoke, curling and swirling behind him. He turned to see that his beautiful bushy tail was on fire. On burning toes, with tail aflame, he quickened his pace down the tree. There was a stream nearby and Possum sat in the cool running waters. He had lost the light. And worse, his splendid tail was pink and bare, never to grow thick and bushy again. An embarrassed Possum returned home. He had failed to bring light.

Buzzard was next to come forward. "Everyone can see I have the finest, thickest feathers on my head." All agreed. Buzzard did have a gorgeous head of feathers. "I will fly to the other side of the world, steal some light and hide it under my feathers. I will return before the people even know it is missing," said Buzzard.

"It could work," said the others.

Buzzard set off for the far side of the world. When he came to the tallest of trees, the tree that held the glowing ball of light, he flew high up into the clouds. He dove straight down into the great shining light. The closer he came, the hotter it grew. With open talons he snatched a bit of light. Stuffing it under the thick feathers on his head, Buzzard started his journey home.

As he flew over a wide lake he smelled something strange. Suddenly he felt terrible pain. Smoke burned his eyes. With flames shooting from his head, Buzzard dove into the waters below. As he rose up from the depths of the lake, Buzzard realized that he had lost the light. And even worse, his head was bald, never again to grow thick beautiful feathers. Embarrassed, he returned home to tell of his failed attempt to bring light.

Now, all the while, Grandmother Spider sat within the thin strands of her web at the top of the world. She had heard the discussion and had seen the failed attempts to bring light. Quick as a flash, on a single delicate strand she dropped down. "I will bring light," she said. As swiftly as she dropped down, Grandmother Spider ascended into her heavenly web. High above the earth she prepared for her journey to the other side of the world.

She fashioned a pot of clay with a snug lid. Although Grandmother Spider took great pride in her beautiful, delicately woven webs, she knew that now she needed a web built more for strength than for beauty. Securing strong strands to the heavenly clouds, she made her way to the other side of the world and to the tallest of trees, the tree that held the glowing ball of light.

Suspended high above the tree, she swiftly lowered herself, holding the clay pot in four tiny, hairy legs, and the lid in another. She snatched a tiny bit of light, put it in the pot, secured the lid, and sped up the strand. Carrying the heavy pot, she returned to the center of her web high above the earth. She removed the lid and poured the light over the dark half of the world.

All the people, animals, and birds, could see! "Thank you Grandmother Spider. You are the wisest of all creatures," they said.

Upon seeing how grateful everyone was, she gave the people two more wonderful gifts. Down the thin strands of her web she sent the art of making beautiful clay pots, and the knowledge of fire.

AFTERWORD

This tapestry of stories is woven with the wonderment of the skyworld and the mysteries it holds. The ancestors told these tales as a way of explaining the vast and ever-changing night sky. They told them under a twinkling canopy of stars with respect, humor, and an overwhelming sense of awe for the endless powers of the universe.

The Wasco, who live along the banks of the Columbia River, tell of a legendary hero, Coyote. He is a vain trickster who uses his magical powers and inventiveness to create the Big Dipper. The migration of snow geese over Coeur d'Alene Lake inspired the Salish story of the constellation known as the Swan. The Ojibwa, living west of the Great Lakes, tell of star visitors, enchanted circles, and human longing. Old Man, the Blackfoot claim, created the plains where they once roamed freely. The creator of all, he is a combination of virtue and folly. As great as his powers may be, his son's are stronger. But Grandmother's wisdom is the strongest when she brings light to the Cherokee.

I hope these stories have awakened your wonder in the glory of the night sky. I hope you enjoyed them as much as I have enjoyed bringing them to you. *Nia wen.* Thank you.

C.J. Taylor